r e b i r t h

by

Jacqueline Favis

rebirth

First Edition 2007

Published by Jacqueline J. Favis ▪ Chicago, IL

ISBN-13: 978-0-6151-6639-1

"The tree of love its roots hath spread

Deep in my heart, and rears its head;

Rich are its fruits: they joy dispense;

Transport the heart, and ravish sense.

In love's sweet swoon to thee I cleave,

Bless'd source of love . . . ,"

-        St. Francis of Assisi

ONE

It was here, before the town was ever an idea. I recall seeing it in the background of great-grandfather's old family picnic photos. A beautiful accent to any image – the town's infamous cherry blossom tree prevailed. Standing glorious, with its branches echoing the sun's pleasant rays, one could stand underneath it and gaze spellbound to its beauty. The pink and white petals emanated calm to any stranger, and left you with such serenity. It stood as always now, standing strong and calm in the bitter breeze. As the surrounding fellow trees were now bare from the heart of winter, this cherry tree... the first oddity I observed that historic day... stood perplexingly – in full bloom.

The sun's glare shone down throughout the tree. So, if you didn't look just right, you may have missed her. I was the first to see her, the second oddity of that remarkable day.

Like a contented bird, balancing on the highest branch, she stood there. But like the tree itself, she radiated such a kindness and warmth. I know I had never seen her in town. But here was this woman, pleasantly smiling, with an upward glance to the heavens. Her face shone like she had a wonderful blessed secret. She was dressed in a gown of white, a shimmering ivory, picking up a variety of pastels. Her feet lay bare, easily and lightly on that top branch. I didn't know what to think of her. Was she ill? Was she an angel? Was she an alien?

I wrapped my coat tighter around me, as I hopped out of my car; I had just finished my final 45-minute drive from the facility. Shading my eyes with my hands from the sun's brilliance, I walked on the grass approaching carefully towards her. Clearing my throat, I questioned, "...hello?" and waited.

Nothing. Not even a glimpse in my direction. She remained in place like a branch of the tree itself. Thinking maybe she hadn't initially heard me, "Uhm.. Miss?"

No reaction. Who was this lady?

Bizarrely, I felt so comforted in her presence. I was beginning to become unaware of the harsh frozen chill this winter had recently brought. She exuded such a peace all throughout me. Numb. Mesmerized. I was like a child being held in a loving mother's embrace. My entire being was feeling lighter than air, as if I were floating a few inches above the ground. Starting out so faintly, I began to feel this docile love; it easily and slowly pulsated towards and through me. The warmth of this feeling spread like an invisible, glowing pleasant shower enveloping me. I knew that some sensational news was being headed my way. And I basked in this growing thrill, feeling marvelous that there was something vitally paramount I would soon be sharing with others. It was a silent message, a knowing. This cherished love was amplifying more and more throughout me; it felt as if there were angelic guides flooding me with an abounding joy of happiness. I stood there, content, observing her and incessantly beaming from this feeling.

§

A crowd had slowly been gathering. My fellow benevolent, good-Samaritan, neighbors had spotted me, erroneously assuming I had been stranded, but one by one followed my stare to the sky as they pulled up. As the onlookers grew, the silent murmurs commenced, with inquisitive looks to the woman in white. Some remained hypnotized, transforming to a state of jubilation and rapture, as I was. Moments later, sirens began their quiet wails from the distance, causing an unwelcome disruption. Someone had called for help.

Officers on the scene, whistled in amazement, as they stepped out of their cars. "Ma'am?" one shouted. "Scuse me – Ma'am?" he questioned.

She gave the same blank acknowledgment. Maybe she was deaf? One continued, with his helpless shrug to his partner, "Ah... Just stay put. We'll get you outta there shortly." He left with an unsure comment. The crowd had parted for the town's dormant firefighters to bring their ladder forward, as the help climbed, looking obviously puzzled by never witnessing a call such as this before.

Only a few began to notice a change in the atmosphere. It wasn't frightening. A calm fog seemed to be making its presence known. The fog, becoming denser, soon made it difficult for me to see barely 10 feet in front of me. Oddly, this vapor positioned itself in a way, so as to not keep children hidden away from their parents – insanely puzzling. Grumbles of annoyance from the emergency crew were heard; orders were put on halt. But as tranquilly as it had arrived, it left – leaving the woman gone as well.

Astounded and startled gasps were heard from the audience upon looking up. People immediately began looking around to see if she was hurt and had fallen, but no one found a remnant of anything that this woman had ever been there. We all stood there, some for almost hours, just wondering... Not only *who was she*, but *why* had she bothered to show herself to us at all? And why had she left some of us with such an unforgettable amiable and enchanting feeling?

§

Tippin Ridge remained a buzz over what had occurred. I considered myself lucky though, that I lived in a down-to-earth community, and we didn't have our church leaders preaching any "Repent! It's the end of the world!" sermons. Further, we didn't have to handle any local gossips giving any of their extreme biased interpretations of what we had witnessed. That evening, as was my journalistic nature, I had settled in after dinner, to watch the evening news.

My heart hammered as my eyes fixed to the set. Shocking screens, channel after channel, displayed similar news clips, about a woman in white – from everywhere! Footage ranged from Washington and Anchorage to London and Nepal. *What was happening?* My after-dinner drink fell lifeless in my throat. Nervous worms squirmed inside me as I absorbed the world-changing chatter. I finally focused in on one of the top worldwide coverage channels, with its endless highlighted words scrolling in red running at the bottom of the screen. I attempted to deeply breathe away the apprehension, putting to use what I learned at the facility: *Inhale... 3 2 1... Hold... Exhale... 3 2 1... Hold...*

In his typical obnoxious "reporter" tone, renowned Philip Jenkins spoke, reporting from an unknown somewhere in South America. "I'm standing here from a remote Brazilian village, where eye witnesses have *claimed* to have seen a woman as dressed in *white*, standing atop a peak of the town's *highest* mountain. Elevation is *noted* at ...″ The gorgeous mountain scene took the camera's attention. With its smooth and jagged cliffs, the mountainous view was gloriously exhilarating yet dared you to not disrespect it. Tiny shacks of some villagers' homes sat gently like adoring butterflies on this volcanic beauty. The villagers were obviously not accustomed to the Western intrusion, yet kindly made any accommodations to the nosy crew. They peered unabashedly at Jenkins and the camera, offering their over-eager responses to his questioning.

I clicked on. Like all the other stations I had surfed through, there was no report of anyone being able to capture a photo of this woman. *How is that possible? No one could capture an image of her? No one in our 6 and a half billion plus population?* However, the next foreign correspondent detailed, "Amateur photographer, Clara Santini, was on the shore at the time shooting a wedding party. She apparently *took* a snapshot of this woman, but the camera appears to have captured nothing... *nothing* but a *mist* where the woman had reportedly been standing." I felt the knots forming in my stomach. *Breathe!* The camera cut away to reveal this novice photo. It was a simple picture of a cloud with the terrain of the land and the San Francisco Bay mixed in. Nothing spectacular was in the shot, except the knowing that immeasurable others had also reported that mysterious mist as well. The cotton candy pink wedding party was gazing upwards in the scene as well. Report after report, my TV flooded with screens of photos with crowds of people, looking upwards, always in some outside nature scene, nationally and internationally. Most faces reassuringly looked calm; however there were those few that occasionally displayed face of fear.

I cuddled down further into the comfort of my down blanket. My mind flew back to my chaotic state many months ago. The multi-colored pills had cursed me with its false, happy delusion. I despised the fact for having ever met up with that ignorant student of mine. All it takes is one taste to get hooked. Never thought that would happen to me. I thought I was always simply strong enough, intellectually and physically, to stay from those reckless addictions. I guess anybody can get hooked. If it was last year right now, I wouldn't be going through this angst alone. *It* would get me through this. ... But rehab taught me to breathe properly. ...*Exhale*...

The news reports continued. I couldn't stop watching. Details ranged from feelings of joy to feelings of fear. One woman stated her feelings. "I... I felt such... such extreme peace! ...and joy!" gasped a British librarian with the immense Buckingham Palace behind her. One Irish gentleman, in a town just on the outskirts of Dublin, angrily spat at the cameras, obviously fearful from his own account, his translation fumed, "She's a devil! She's evil!!" But countless others from other countries were stating a similar, apathetic and nonchalant statement, shrugging, "...I don't know... nothing… I felt nothing..."

I wanted – intended! – involvement in this world-changing event!

TWO

8 months earlier…

As Dean of UFN, James was a pleasant site around campus. His tall and lanky build, masked with his rimless, rectangular frames, and enormous, broad smile produced the illusion of a brilliant, yet affable professor. Middle-age was slowly fading away from him, but he still had the vitality of a young, pleasing professor starting out. His adoring wife, despite the silver in his air, couldn't suppress her amusement, referring to him as her very own "James Dean."

He was as usual walking briskly from one end of the campus to another; today it was from the Engineering to the English department. It was one of those perfect weather days, mildly sunny with a shy breeze. He took this opportunity to get in a 15-minute walk. Chatting with Dr. Terryl, they enthusiastically discussed the high points of the latest professor they had been interviewing for the empty "ENG 210 – English Renaissance Literature" teaching spot. Since Professor Reed's desk was enroute, they decided to pop in for a surprise to get his input as well. Tanner Reed had finished conducting a 2-hour interview with the gentleman only yesterday, and James wanted to concur that he as well had felt equally optimistic.

Knocking as if he were king of the castle and needn't have bothered, James entered Tanner's tiny mouse hole of an office. Typical of most professors, it was surrounded with mounds of student papers and teaching books on literature and journalism; piles towered high in every spare corner of the jungled room. A small window with its dusty blinds hid behind his desk.

"Hey Tanner!" James announced, dragging Dr. Terryl's short stature along side. "Bother you for a sec?" He caught the young professor behind his desk popping a pill, mumbling about a "student migraine."

"Sure, sure, c'mon in..." Tanner replied, distracted, motioning helplessly to any place that one could stand with nonexistent guest chairs. Before anyone could relax however, Tanner's TA, Sandra, popped in briefly with an interruption for him. "One minute..." he said to the two men, holding up an index finger to excuse him from their presence. She was about to teach one of his Common Core classes, "Creative and Critical Thinking," in five minutes, so he wanted to be sure she had a final grasp on things.

Left in the room, James, wanting to jot down a few notes, scrambled to find a notepad – or any scrap of paper – off of Tanner's frazzled desk. Terryl was too busy commenting further on the interviewee, while James inattentively responded an agreement, fumbling for a futile pen search in Tanner's desk drawers.

He stopped. His eye instantly caught the assorted blue and purple pills in their shiny, perforated casing. Without hesitation, he knew what they were, recalling his illegally "fun" days of his youth. Shutting the drawer, Terryl hadn't noticed James fleeting disturbed face.

"Sorry 'bout that..." Tanner said, squeezing back in the room, mobilizing behind his desk. James attempted to remain calm during the following minutes on the prospect's discussion. It would only be an hour or so later that he came back to Tanner's office, alone –

parentally handing him a letter of suspension along with a notice of mandatory rehabilitation. Within a few days, it was public knowledge amongst the staff as to what happened to their fellow colleague.

THREE

Restlessness took over me that night. I had this strong desire to solve this puzzle. After having felt her kind presence, I knew she had left me a message to participate in some meaningful role. The university was already aware of my year-long tenure, and after calling up James, I could use my leave to continue and devote my research into this news-worthy piece. Unless you were in complete isolation, this international unexplainable phenomenon was on the mouths and minds of all.

I thus decided to call upon my buddy, Professor Charlie Lange. He was currently in Italy, teaching around the San Marino region. I was ecstatic when he shared my enthusiasm about my unexpected visit.

"Absolutely, Tanner!" It was so wonderful to hear my old friend's boisterous voice again. "Just send me the details of your flight." I briefly informed him of my intent to perform research into unraveling the particulars of this peculiar woman. I didn't confess to my friend having already seen the woman and felt her altruistic aura. But I would definitely share it with him in person, wanting him to truly see my honest expression. He knew about my recent affairs, and I didn't want him thinking I was under any influence.

If anyone would understand my eagerness, it would be him. Some of the more conservative academic staff at the university had disproved of Charlie's teaching style. Charlie had a unique way of teaching his students. He would encourage them to explore their journalism "independently". He was very hands-free and non-micro managerial towards their fresh minds. Ironically, he didn't want to *teach* at all, but rather he wanted these unsullied minds to research and report on stories on their own, without becoming robotic to some mundane pattern on how maybe they *should* report. He refused to have his students become Philip Jenkins clones. Naturally, this also instigated the more apathetic students to write nonsensical, ludicrous columns and papers. Then, they would go on the defensive and blame Charlie of his lack of discipline and not having the proper scholastic guidance. However, it also enticed the more discerning, brilliant students to pursue outrageous yet legitimate stories. These students went on to become his beloved infamous broadcasters, columnists and commentators to some of the more prominent national newspapers and press associations. Thus, not many dared to oust the eccentric Professor Charlie Lange from the school.

The exhilaration of this new journey was building inside of me! I immediately purchased a handy journal to chronicle all the events I would soon discover, deciding it may be best not to lumber along my cumbersome laptop in case any defect with the equipment were to occur. I squeezed the camel leather-bound journal in my hands. This also would facilitate my passing through various airports' security I may encounter I rationed. Not knowing how long my venture would take, I packed one suitcase, filling it to the seams with a variety of clothes – who knew if the weather would change depending on the length of my stay? I called up my parents, a few close relatives and friends informing them of a "little European getaway."

I set on purchasing my one-way flight.

§

I attempted to settle in comfortably for the eight-and-a-half hour's long flight. It had only been a few days since the woman's appearance, but already people were talking. The plane was a jitter with endless opinions on what they heard from their distant cousin from the West coast to their email pals from down South. The elderly lady sitting on my left captured my interest however. I was about to position the dollar plastic headphones into my ears to hear some garbled Beethoven. My seating companion had other intentions. Obviously comfortable with whoever her fellow passenger seatmate would be, the small, gentle woman placed a soft, kind hand on my arm, initially remarking, "So, honey, where were *you* when the *appearances* began?" her eyes enlarging when emphasizing on the word 'appearances'.

She was adorable, reminding me of my late nana. I turned to face her, clearing my throat, confidentially informing her I had in fact seen her in person, relating my account of the tree in my town. "Oh! – A tree? How fascinating!" she responded, gripping my arm a little tighter from exuberance. But it really wasn't as fascinating as where she herself had seen the woman. I politely asked her if she too had seen the lady or just heard all the news. Beaming like a teapot that's reached its maximum boiling point, she spoke as a child sharing an astounding secret. "...yes!..." she whispered with a controlled thrill.

She smiled, gazing up at nothing in particular. "...Oh it was so remarkable...," she continued. "There I was, getting our church newsletters ready for mass... I work at St. Agatha you see... And –" with a quick slap on my arm "there was such a commotion heard outdoors! ...

Well, of *course* I wanted to be sure everything was alright." I nodded a humble agreement. "So I headed out those doors as quickly as these two slow feet could move!" she laughed.

"... And there she was!" she said with dramatic pause. "Oh my, my, my..." she giggled. "I couldn't believe what I was seeing!"

I perked, "What was it?"

"Well now... It will sound a bit bizarre." She hesitantly said, obviously now cautious, not wanting to appear delusional, "But... there was this expansive rainbow – now, not just a simple after-the-storm kind – oh no, this one extended to who knows where from who knows where! My... the colors were so deep and clear and – oh! I just have never seen such intense colors! ... We could only see the middle of the rainbow, and balanced, like a delicate flower, was her!" It was hard not to get caught up in the woman's tale, although sounding something out of a children's fairy tale novel. The rest of her narrative continued on sounding similar to my own account – the gaze upwards, the fog. There had to be a story somewhere.

Meanwhile, I heard a man behind us snicker and grumble, "Psh... Crazy lady..." Fortunately, the sweet woman didn't hear him. She eventually fell quickly asleep, as a toddler who'd been at a playground all day with no nap. I jotted down her story in my journal, my first enticing entry, "February, 8th..." She kindly gave me permission later to use those details for my research, but embarrassedly asking that I simply use her first initial and last name only.

Only two hours more until we reached Rimini...

rebirth   *JF*

FOUR

Moody, Eric: Prison #03649788, Attempted
Robbery.

The melancholy bars clanged shut for another
night. He stretched himself in a languorous
manner onto the cheap and flattened mattress.
It would be two years tomorrow and yet he
still, quite proudly, refused to acknowledge his
obvious guilt in the crime. The despondent
clergymen that would occasionally visit him
steadily dwindled on participating in any
further intervention.

His cell became cloudy. ... Eric found himself
in a downpour. He was running on a glassy
sidewalk. He needed to make an imperative
stop at the ATM to surprise her for their
anniversary dinner. The splattering irritancy
upon his umbrella-less face blurred his vision

from the stranger hidden in the alleyway. Upon reaching the machine, his hand grabbed for his wallet and swiftly he slid the card, soon dashing for the bills released. A sudden force pummeled his head onto the unaffected steel of the ATM machine. Unforgiving boots thrust unremittingly into his ribs. He groaned, collapsing onto the rough, wet pavement and gagged as he felt the salty liquid begin to choke in his mouth.

He heard a kind assistance from across the street yelling over their cellphones to the operators. Gentle souls stayed with him until the squad and ambulance arrived. It was a blessing there were people around who were able to restrain his arrogant attacker. When the cops shoved the aggressor into the backseat, he struggled to get a look at his face. A frightened stun ran through him.

It was himself, his own face that glared back.

FIVE

It was a beckoning image that met my eyes, as the plane began its descent. I had never been to another country, except to Canada for a brief teaching visit during her frigid months. I was overcome with a controlled happy frantic at being in a new land. I observed a hilly region, filled with its domestic, agreeable homes. Its old world quality made me ponder on how I would be welcomed into their implied charmed world.

Rimini was the seaside city we flew into. From there, it would be another 15 minute drive into San Marino. Through the thick airplane window, I had made out some of the glorious landscape. Many beautiful beaches were seen, and like the miniature reflections of the clouds above, the cottony white surface of the boater's sails skimmed along in the buoyant friendly waves. A variety of hotels lined the beachside, loaded with their adventurous tourists. Deeper into the land, the slopes relaxed into more of the peaceful greenery of the rolling hills and vineyards. A few traditional, ancient buildings popped up throughout the scene.

The bump of the plane hitting ground awoke me from my spellbound state. It wasn't long before I gathered my meager belongings, impatient to see how my friend had changed.

§

Charlie hadn't changed much at all. In fact, his sabbatical had blessed him with a more energized, youthful appearance. He must have been eating healthier, for he did not have as much weight on as he once had. However, he still managed to give me his familiar barbarous embrace, shouting, "Tanner!" He was dressed, as always, in khaki camping shorts and his faded, white hiking hat. His gray, straggly beard made its poor attempt to look well-groomed. We briefly chatted about our long overdue reunion as I grabbed my luggage; he decided we should en route to a local restaurant, Caffe Zanni.

They had an assortment of fresh fish meals. It was a relaxed ambience, with pleasant light classical music of the local culture, playing in the background. Taking one of Charlie's suggestions off the menu, I reveled in the scent and savor of my dinner. The naturally-made, delicious and yet unusual taste of their cold gelato was the perfect complement to finish off this exquisite meal.

Charlie had maintained busy working at a top local newspaper there, doing some minor editorial and proofreading work. His devotion was more to exploring the country's historical landmarks. Anything from the radiant, classical cathedrals to the desolate, bleak, historic battle sites, he nose-dived into uncovering hidden, obscure and unique stories of those times.

At an uncommon lull in our conversation, I inserted my lead-in regarding the woman at the cherry tree. Leaning forward in a clandestine pose, I proceeded to disclose to my friend what had overcome me that day.

"...Well...fascinating as St. Catherine's may have been, you won't believe what happened when I drove back to Tippen Ridge..." Seeing I finally had the attention of my loquacious colleague, I went on to describe the details of how I had come upon her, after my last day of rehab. I set up the atmosphere of that day's events and bluntly stated, "But it was more than seeing with your eyes... I began to honestly feel so... I'm not sure how to explain it. ...Just so... loved? It was as if there were a million invisible angelic spirits hovering all around me ... through me ... sending me ...like... happy *vibrations*???" As I spoke my words, I hoped my friend didn't think I had regressed to my old habits. But Charlie, knowing my critical and sometimes scientific mental stability, believed me and sat astounded in my animation. It felt comforting to confess to someone that I also was one of those onlookers who had actually felt something that day.

§

Built of stone and brick, the home Charlie was renting, from a fellow journalist, embodied a cheerful and commodious abode. The three-bedroom dwelling would be occupied by

Charlie, and Aida, an arduous older live-in housemaid, and I. Located on a placid hillside, it lent me a picturesque view of the San Marino landscape.

My companion had retired for the evening, claiming an early morning and mumbling on traffic conditions. Although Aida had graciously prepared my bed and towels for me, I toured the quiet, quaint home, and found the open dining and living room areas bidding me to relax on its burgundy leather recliner. I found the same local paper, which Charlie had shown me at the restaurant, scattered in pieces on the coffee table. I grabbed the Editorials section and began to read more of other revelations local and worldwide.

It was an anonymous letter from an ex-military personnel, residing as a prisoner in Australia, for war crimes he had committed. The article included verbatim what was submitted.

"...I walked into the fog... and was suddenly in the past. I was in some type of prison, the kind I had usually forced my enemies into. Only this time... I played the role of the opposition ...the victim. ... I felt their emotions, I felt how my prisoner...how much he missed and loved his family, I felt truly that *I* was *him*. ... You don't understand: the emotions I felt were 100-fold what one would normally feel! It was intense. I no longer was myself. The situation... continued where I was so cruelly hurt. I felt the actual physical pain of every frightening situation – the cold and fierce torture room, the loneliness, the darkness of the cell... the physical and mental attacks forced upon me. ... I felt myself ... die?. ... As this person, I died... I felt peace. I saw the funeral! I was feeling all of their emotions – this man's family – their pain and hurt of losing their son... their great sadness... their tears... their overwhelming grief. I realized again who had caused such agony:

I saw myself...

But it didn't end there. ... The dream continued: I was now myself again, realizing what I had done. I passed a stranger mumbling good riddance and tossing his newspaper aside. I glanced at it only to see my picture... my death date.

The scene, this experience, changed once again. I was facing another circumstance where I had hurt someone.

Again this cycle continued... with all those I've hurt.

You don't understand. No. This just wasn't some dream I had. I actually felt – it was palpable and psychological – everything I did. The feelings are still so ingrained within me till now.

It was my hell."

§

I laid the paper down, temporarily absorbing his emotions and fear. I couldn't believe what I had just read. It was bizarre, frightening. I swiftly jotted down, in my journal, the prisoner's sad tale.

I continued on reading a few other melancholic narratives. It saddened me when reading of how there were also countless guilty prisoners experiencing and reliving their own victim's rapes and murders and feeling every physical and mental sensation. It must have been self-loathing to in the end see their own faces or know that it was themselves who had caused so much pain. There were however, those prisoners, who had had similar charges but had already confessed previously and had been bettering themselves, and were grateful to have experienced none of this guilt and sorrow their fellow captives had undergone.

My eyes roamed onward. From China, a woman had submitted her own account. The interpretation was translated as follows:

"… I saw her… She was beautiful…delicate… A gentle whiteness began to wisp around me. I continued walking. … I was somewhere familiar, an occurrence from my past. But, I was someone else… I began to absorb all of this man's emotions – all the love he felt to his wife and children, all the indifference and annoyance to his coworkers as well. ... I felt a pain in my heart, physical. It was hard to breathe. I was scared but somehow knew I was safe. I passed out and awoke in a hospital.

A very kind nurse helped me rehabilitate. I did not see her face. She was the only one on that staff who sincerely took the time to help me. She truly cared. I felt many days pass, as I lay in this hospital, recovering. She was always there...so kind, so soothing, so affectionate... I felt so very loved. The feeling of care and love was so strong. I was so overcome. It was overpowering! The emotions were extreme.
It was my final day in that hospital and I finally saw who she was. I was dumbfounded. I was in shock. That nurse... I saw her face... she was ME!

I continued throughout this "fog" – it was so much more than a dream – reliving all the good I have done and how it had affected others. ... I eventually "awoke" still feeling these extreme good emotions. It was wondrous.... monumental!"

§

I was elated with her story and added to my journal "February 9th... We are all being dealt an important teaching here. Perhaps only those that are being affected by the fog have lived a life that has so *strongly* affected others? – beneficially or detrimentally?"

§

For his growling stomach, Charlie got up at midnight. He stumbled blindly to the kitchen. His hand grabbed a box of something salty in the darkened counter, but it fell, tumbling all around him. He growled having to turn on the light, protecting his eyes from the unpleasant, fluorescent glare.

On the kitchen floor, he saw, disheartened: a familiar blue pill.

SIX

It was my second fog experience.

After doing some more of the mundane tourist activities during my initial days in San Marino, I had decided to venture out into some of the more isolated areas of the country. Charlie had an appointment with a fellow reporter from the paper to discuss more on one of the local cathedral's middle age history, and so I had been left that day on my own to explore. I took one of their buses to a beautiful landscape, vineyards in the distance populated by occasional olive trees. I began walking along the dirt road, not knowing where it would lead me too.

As I heedlessly strolled, my mind began to wander on how I would find further details on this lady. My preoccupied mind failed to notice what was occurring around me.

Ever so gently, I was gradually being encompassed by a hazy mist. When I first noticed it, I immediately knew what was going to occur – something incredible! My initial human reaction, for an infinitesimal second, was to halt with an apprehensive gasp of paranoia. But my anxiety was instantly replaced with one of calm and silent harmonious serenity. Breathing deeply, I continued walking forward. As expected, the mist became denser, but I felt protected and guided in my path.

I'm not sure what I expected to see, but I felt that it would have been a similar affair to what I had heard those others encountered – feeling and experiencing some pleasant (or unpleasant) situation from their past.

But this was anything but.

I found myself standing on the shore of a majestic and wondrous beach. The lulling sound of the inhale and exhale of the ocean waved in rhythm with my breath. I looked to both the left and to the right and could see no end to this shore. It was a limitless, ageless coast with its pure white sand.

Looking down, almost losing my balance, it was then I noticed I was barefoot. How? My feet squished around a few moments in this pleasantly warm mix of dry and wet sand. I began to walk, but when I walked, I felt as if I were floating a few inches above ground, in a dreamlike state. Each step I took in that light, slow motion and magnetic shift made me pause and savor every remarkable step. Upon reaching the water, it tenderly brushed the tepid water of foam and waves through my feet.

Peering into the ocean itself was a breathtaking site. I could see a variety of spectacular colorful sea creatures for miles with unlimited depth, the color so immensely clear and blue. Sea green turtles and flighty sea horses mixed in cordially with gleeful dolphins and tangerine-orange koi. Scattered magenta, bright yellow and baby blue sea coral beautified the image further. Just as awe-inspiring, the view skywards was miraculously grand. Simultaneously filled with midnight stars and a stunning sun, my individuality could not comprehend this marvelous coexistence.

I stood there, enjoying the repose feeling. Truly, I was without a care in the world.

Back in the sunlit-midnight sky, sheers of light began to extend from above and cradle my being in ultimate, consummate bliss. I wasn't afraid. I felt as if my whole being were light, and I was being acknowledged and welcomed back to a sense of... home.

§

During that experience, I briefly thought 'Have I died?' I cannot fully comprehend how I came out of that state. I instantly began filling pages of what had occurred and what teachings had filled my being ("February 17th..."). My mind and heart began a fuller understanding of what was recently occurring: Our world was transforming; we were evolving. It was undergoing a new birth. An imprint, awareness, had been left in my mind: that world I had seen was really our future world, beyond some tens of thousands of years.

SEVEN

Travone, Neil: Burglary.

Neil knew he was no longer himself. The essence of Maya Lee was filling his own being. It was uncanny and terrifying to feel his self changing – let alone to someone of the opposite gender. Her mind became his. He instantly knew everything about her, becoming her – he absorbed all her own beliefs, likes and dislikes, factual and not. He felt himself as her. The love she felt for her children, her husband, her family... He felt it with an abnormal force.

He, as Maya, was heading to work. He was there, opening the doors, the first to arrive. He knew everything – where the new accounts were filled, how to handle the drive-thru customers, what the lock combination was for the main safe. He felt her undying loyalty to the company.

The events happened too quickly to comprehend. He saw himself. He was yelling and pointing the gun, but as her, he was too paralyzed to move. The gun went unquestionably off. He felt her pain, physically. He felt the bullet tearing cruelly through her chest. He was experiencing the affect of his own regrettable burden. The sharp pain was unnoticeable at first but grew to an excruciating hellish ferocity, suffocating his breath. With seizure-like struggles, he fought against the bullet's impending death with spasmodic inhalation. Feeling the excessive, overflow of love to her family, his mind overwhelmed with the forlorn of no longer being with them. Her racing mind knew she would no longer be there for her daughter's wedding, and retiring to the snowy mountain's beauty with her spouse. He underwent all that

his bank robbery had caused.

rebirth   *JF*

EIGHT

Charlie was still dumbfounded by finding the pill. He thought for sure Tanner's 10-month rehab should have provided some beneficial help by now. It was not even a month that he had left the facility. He flushed down the pill last night.

Sadly though, he could not focus on his friend's apparent setback. His mind was lost in thought, filled with the pathetic employment he currently held.

Tanner, like many of his other colleagues back home, was oblivious to Charlie's new work status in Rimini. They were all simply too bedazzled by the fact that he was working in a charming foreign country to fully realize that he was instead yearning for his comfortable home back in the States. It was intensely

competitive to get any reporting job in Rimini –
he was challenged with new graduates, a harsh
job market, as well as the language hurdle he
was yet undertaking. Thus, he ended up
settling for a pitiful meager job, equivalent to a
sad intern back home, with its equally dismal
salary. He refused to admit to anyone,
especially his friends and family back home,
his true circumstances. Thus, he plastered on a
bogus smile of delight whenever he was not at
the newspaper, communicating a "Don't you
wish you were me?" demeanor.

He struggled endlessly in trying to either
establish a name for himself and move up in
the little company, or find a higher paying
position. But there really was no use for an
American journalist there, especially one who
failed to fully comprehend the language.
Nobody enjoyed hearing a report via a
translator's basic rendition. He was amazed
every month though that he was able to

produce enough income to cover the house payment. One light was that he was able to curb the grocery intake and thus, gave the illusion that he was healthier by his weight loss.

He falsely gave Tanner and others the impression he was out covering some newsworthy piece, when in fact, those were the assignments the more notable reporters were currently covering.

An unexpected visitor one day popped in to see his unlucky sort, making an intriguing proposition. Nothing extraordinary stood out about this gentleman. A plain commoner one would simply overlook in a crowded street. To anyone looking, they would never have known he had a mind intelligent and gifted, yet cunning and manipulative as well. This man was a loner. He only befriended fools he knew that could provide him whatever he sought. This was a man who did his research, who planned and plotted on these unfortunate individuals, discovering their weaknesses and mischievously used them to his advantage. As a meticulous planner would note, his mind thought 'Next victim: Charlie Lange.'

Charlie was busy wrapping up an interview with the latest popular chef to pop up in the downtown plaza. He was casually approached by the simple man as he finished typing in some last-minute notes.

"Excuse me... Mr. Lange?" a kind voice spoke.

Charlie looked up curiously. "Yes?" he said with a smile, his hands busily packing up his papers. The man held out his hand. Charlie automatically extended, shaking his, questioning, "I'm sorry – " wondering who this man was and if he should have known him.

"I'm a fan." The man said eagerly. 'A fan?' Charlie's mind asked. 'Well, that's a first.' he thought. Charlie was taken aback and, flattered, smiled. The *fan* continued on, expounding on Charlie's latest articles and a few almost-forgotten ones, pointing out what he found so intriguing about Charlie's interviews and style. Finally, giving Charlie a break, he managed to interrupt with a grateful and too-honest, "Well, thanks! Glad to get noticed!" The man went on still. Charlie discovered his interest in developing his own writing as well. He thought, as a journalist working with one of the well-known papers, Charlie had the skill to critique this man's writing. They set a later time and date for coffee.

The man thought, leaving happily with a smirk, 'Foot in the door. Check. Next, gain trust.'

NINE

As planned, I made my way to Pamiera Plaza
to meet up with Charlie. He was apparently at
the latest exhibit in the downtown museum,
conducting interviews with the top artists and
sculptors whose pieces were to be displayed.
Managing somehow with my extremely basic
knowledge of the language, I managed to get a
bus and taxi ride back into the area. Paying the
smiling driver – most likely scamming me out
of a more-than-required fee – I hopped out of
the car taking in the busy view.

I was on a sidewalk, my eyes before a wide
semi-circular street. It was a combination of a
modern and old world appearance. The town,
where it could, maintained much historical
structure as possible. The main street and the
alleyways were diverse with the current clean
pavements as well as cobblestone streets in

other paths. The plaza was busy with the typical tourists flashing their cameras in awe, the food merchants selling to the hot pedestrians, and business men and women heading to and from their office buildings. Beautiful parks, the historical museum, a grand cathedral, office buildings, quaint shops and top restaurants all jumbled the landscape.

I made myself comfortable on one of the park benches, as Charlie's interview time was still I believed not quite finished, and massaged my feet from my busy day. I wanted to ponder further on what I had been through. My eyes were about to close when I spotted an alluring dessert stand nearby. I thought I could manage to get something with what little the cab driver had *not* managed to rob from me. As I walked towards the stand, I heard my name being called. Charlie was waving, heading down the museum steps. I diverted my plan and headed in the direction of my friend instead.

Without warning, my feet began to wobble. My mind didn't realize it at first, but it was the ground that began to tremble. Frantically, I looked at my friend, who surprisingly, seemed oblivious to what was happening. I was about to yell over to him, when I noticed further the entire plaza scene was ...*odd*. Charlie was walking outside of the building ever so casually, continuing to smile towards me. I began to notice others around me. Some were reacting hysterically, while others continued on, unaware of this sudden earthquake. It was bizarre! My body felt dizzy. It felt as if I was being torn in half. As the earth continued to rumble beneath me, I saw the historic structures losing their balance. Alongside Charlie were a group of children, returning back to school from a field trip. The giggly bunch was bouncing back to the bus, carefree. I wanted to scream out to them to hurry and find safety instead; however, things appeared perfectly safe to them. I couldn't understand how. I saw a window burst a couple floors above them. The shattered glass about to pierce anything it sought below. I froze, terrified as to what I would see. I cowardly covered my eyes and prepared myself to hear the screams of the children. But... I heard nothing. I looked. The glass had fallen, but the children were boarding their bus with no fuss whatsoever! I watched their little feet walk *through* the glass. I gulped a panicked breath. 'Was I dead??? Were *they* dead?' my mind could not comprehend this confusion. I cautiously and slowly made my way back to the bench. I grabbed a hold of the back trying to keep myself stable. I saw the beautiful cathedral begin to collapse. The striking doorway entrance tore in half, collapsing in two, bringing the floor above it roaring down upon itself. I heard screams of a few ill-fated people and witnessed heavy structures crumble and crash downwards; my stomach sickened as I saw some poor souls standing on the sidewalk being crushed. But I also saw a few priests walk past them and right *through* them! I was dizzy. What was happening?

Everything went black.

§

My body felt tired. It seemed as if I were asleep a hundred years. I felt myself on a stiff bed, starchy sheets. I forced my eyes to open. I saw Charlie, asleep in a chair next to me. I looked around. I was in a hospital. I had an IV hooked up to me, probably thinking dehydration made me pass out. I began to recall the chaotic plaza scene. What had really happened? Charlie could tell me, hopefully. Meanwhile, I leaned back on the white sheets and decided to not disturb my friend. I closed my eyes desiring a deep sleep away from these odd scenes.

TEN

Carr, Sophia: Betrayal.

She had a nonchalant attitude when it came to anyone she met – lovers, friends, even her devoted felines. Her relationship with Jeremy was passionate, yet obviously one-sided. She was his first love; he was her umpteenth love. ... The fog rolled by one afternoon. The exchange of leaving her awareness and transforming into his felt so abnormal at first. But she became slowly and progressively more infused with all his loves – his dying father, his love of fishing, and his passion for her. She felt his high-strung, puppy-love emotion upon joyously getting her to say "yes" on a cappuccino date. She felt all his zealous affection to every aspect of their dating – their first handholding, first kiss, first trip to Naples. She felt his exuberant happiness as he entered the jewelry shop. His hands had fingered lovingly the engagement ring – the colorless, 3-carat, marquis diamond blazed brilliantly back at him. He was going to surprise her at her work; she felt his intentions. His foolish eagerness bounced his way to her downtown building. He had told her he was on business that Friday. She felt as his hand was crushing the burgundy velvet box in fervor.

He saw her before she saw him. She knew what was coming. She tried to make herself feel indifference, but his passionate emotion dominated. She was having a trivial affair with the egotistical ass who managed the fashion department the floor below hers. He knew him – she had introduced him at the company party last Christmas. They were holding hands, laughing mischievously. She felt, as him, his hands dumbly release the excited grip

on the box. She had been clueless of his
intentions that day.

ELEVEN

Evening had fallen by the time I had woken up from a long rest. Charlie was no longer in the bedside chair. Allowing myself a few minutes to recuperate, I then pushed myself up to see if possibly there was anything on the news that had occurred. I was careful not to mix up the nurse-call button with the remote and clicked the TV on.

A well-dressed, white-haired man was reciting today's news. My ears awaited to hear news on the terrifying earthquake. ... It wasn't the first story. *Odd*... The poised reporter continued on. ... No mention of anything on their second story. Nor their third! *I'm losing it... What in the world happened back there?* I was frustrated, puzzled, angered... I knew what I had seen. But my eyes were shocked to see the news scene focus on folks elegantly dressed for the night's art exhibit. The museum was still there, in one piece.

The door to my room opened and Charlie walked in carrying a cup of coffee. "Hey buddy..." he brightened, seeing me awake. "Gave me a scare earlier."

"...what happened?" my tired voice asked. Charlie made his way back to the chair, cautiously setting down the steaming cup on the table.

"...well..." he got comfortable. "Not sure. ... Maybe you had too much heat today? Were you out long in Marino?" I didn't bother telling him about the second fog incident. It just might push him to move me into *another* type of hospital instead. He mumbled something about the doctors thinking it was just dehydration and that I had passed out.

"Not really... I was maybe out walking for an hour or so." I hesitated before continuing. Charlie gave a clueless shrug. "Charlie... What happened in the plaza? ...Did you see *that*?"

"What happened?" he asked. *Ok folks, I'm nuts!* Maybe my drug use was having some really bad residual affects. "Oh-oh! Yeah," he winked, "Some of those artists do perform a little bizarre if you ask me," he guessed. *No my friend, that's not what I'm talking about.* I laughed in agreement as Charlie turned his attention back to the TV. I couldn't keep this to myself. With all of the latest worldly events occurring every day, surely what I would share couldn't be dismissed?

"Umm... listen..." I waited until he had finished hearing a piece wrap up on the exhibit. His eyes facing me, I questioned, "You didn't see anything odd at the plaza? Nothing?"

"What do you mean exactly?" his friend wondered.

"...Something weird happened back there, Charlie," I bluntly stated. "Really, *really* weird."

"What happened??? Oh! Did you see that woman again??" he asked eagerly, referring to that mystery woman in white.

"No... No...It wasn't her." I replied, shaking my head. "What exactly happened when you saw me?"

He shrugged. "Nothing really. I was heading out of the museum. Saw you. And then just saw you keel over," he motioned, with a sound of a *kerplunk*. "Figured you just had had too much heat..." He rambled on about people helping me, getting an ambulance, paramedics taking me to St. Lucia's; nothing at all about a richter-8 earthquake or collapsing buildings.

I shook my head in disbelief not sure what to make of all of it. I didn't understand it. My friend leaned in and sympathetically asked, "What?"

"...Well...I saw... I felt... Well, there was an earthquake. The ground was shaking. It was bad. It had to be a 7 or 8!" I exclaimed with enlarged eyes. "I saw you... ...and-and those kids! – on that field trip? I saw all of you! But you were all just walking, *walking* out of the museum. It was as if you didn't see anything, *feel* anything, going on." I looked at him for confirmation, and he replied with a confused, unnecessary apologetic shrug.

"…No huh?... Nothing?…"

"…mmm…" My friend shook his head. "Sorry pal… Are you sure you just weren't maybe hallucinating? Seeing things? Cause of the heat?"

"No, no!" I wasn't crazy. I forced myself to calm down. "No… really… I saw it. …the church…falling… the museum…" How could I have been the only one to see that? Feel that?

"I'm sorry man… I don't know…" Charlie responded, really not knowing what to make of it. He knew his friend wasn't in the habit of lying. He had a sudden idea though. A friend of his who could possibly help out: Dr. Roman Montecchio.

§

It wasn't quite a confirmation to my sanity, but hopefully Charlie's friend could provide some help to me. As we left the hospital, Charlie had called up Roman. They made plans to meet with the gentleman the following night, who was leading an assembly at St. Anna's church. Roman was a man, like Tanner, that was becoming deeply involved in the mysteries surrounding all these strange events.

TWELVE

The hall was congested. Engulfed with local reporters and their cameramen, divergent religious leaders, parents hugging their children, professionals and the poor, St. Anna's had not a spare seat to be found. Charlie and I were able to squeeze ourselves and maneuver to a decent area, obtaining a decent view of the podium.

A well-dressed middle-aged gentleman, wearing a non-overpowering navy suit, advanced to the microphone. He introduced himself as Dr. Roman Montecchio, a physicist who was an infamous board member from the University of Milan. Standing just a bit under 5'5", Dr. Montecchio was a man of slight, almost frail, build, displaying a faint ashen beard. Adjusting his charcoal-rimmed spectacles, he monotonously read his note cards with repose. With the occasional exception of a child's yawning complaint of boredom or hunger, the crowd remained hushed. He proceeded to lecture in his scholarly eloquence of his background and desired research into these current events.

Volunteers from the audience bravely participated, relating their joyous stories. Charlie was desperately craving for me to be one of those participants as well. I thought I had caught Roman briefly roll his eyes at one point, but I dismissed it thinking the man must simply be tired. After what felt like hundreds of seemingly genial testimonials poured through, there was remarkably a break in the hands of volunteers hoisting up. I uneasily took that opportunity to impart my own version but to Charlie's displeasure, quickly lowered my hand.

With the final speech, Dr. Montecchio courteously ended the seminar. His focus was quickly upon Tanner and me, and as folks were departing, he fervently extended his hand and motioned me forward. Not being one to squelch his enthusiasm, Charlie tail-gated me to the stage.

Welcoming his hand out to me, Roman greeted me warmly. He was greatly intrigued by what Charlie had told him happened to me. Roman acknowledged my friend with a kind nod. The crowd was lessening, and we made our way to a room outside of the large auditorium.

"Please, please... Come... Sit down..." said the small man. We sat comfortably on old maroon leather chairs in the church secretary's office. He offered us some of the hour old coffee, but we politely refused with a "oh, no thanks" and a wave of our hands.

"So – what did you think?" he sat opposite us behind the large mahogany desk, looking like a child sitting there. He was referring to his finished assembly.

"Yeah… well… wow! It's… something…" I said, not knowing if he believed these testimonials or not. I knew I believed them.

"Indeed." He briefly responded. "So then, Charlie told me about what you saw at the plaza?" he was implying for my response.

"Yes…" I cleared my throat. And related, uneventfully, what I had seen. How I had seen some individuals hurt, some not, but then how I had blacked out. "What do you make of it?" I asked, hoping for some answer.
"Honestly – I don't know." Some help he was. "However…" He searched for a folder in one of the desk's massive drawers. He pulled out a

manila folder, opening it up, displaying some sheets of, it seemed, other individuals. "I have been corresponding with other people, who… like yourself…" he glanced up at me, "…have felt, seen… situations similar." He pulled out two sheets. One had the name and picture of an "Ajani Mbele" and another name and picture of a "Zarina Azalia." Laying a small hand on these sheets he commented, "I'm actually making plans to go visit these two – Ajani and Zarina." He handed me the sheets, allowing me to read further on these two strangers.

What I could quickly gather was that Ajani was a young gentleman from South Africa, and Zarina was a physician in Greece. Roman, meticulous about keeping his own papers in order, invited me, "So after Charlie here told me about your story, I was wondering if you would not like to accompany me to visit them?"

I held back my excitement. Of course I would be! Charlie gratefully interjected my enthusiasm and voted myself in. "Yes – absolutely," I added.

"Great, great..." he jotted down a few notes. "I'll send you the details of my proposed itinerary..." he busily spoke, not looking up. I noticed the doctor sure had a quirky manner about him – desiring to be in control of everything. A call interrupted our meeting, and Roman excused himself for a minute. However, after realizing it would be awhile, he had to bring our meeting to an end. Briefly apologizing, he declared that he would be calling me soon to work out the details. Charlie and I left – eager, wondering what the upcoming destination would be.

§

My body was not prepared for the shock of the African heat after experiencing the severe winter back in the States. Our plane had landed about an hour ago, and Roman and I were still awaiting Ajani's arrival. Roman had called, as he had said, a few days after our meeting. Generously, he worked out all the details: my flight ticket, our hotel stay, etc. Unfortunately, Roman's invitation did not extend to Charlie as well. But my amiable pal wished me well on this next venture, as he mumbled about his upcoming projects.

The South African environment was chaotic with smoke from haggard jeeps and sand-encrusted busses. The people ranged in a mix of a few safari tourists to children in their plaid uniforms to those in immaculate white-robed clothing from head to toe. Barefoot little children were happily and animatedly following us, innocently expecting us to give them (monetary) gifts. However, two University professors currently idle from work could not hand out as much as we would have desired.

A worn white jeep, with its sun-beaten faded leather seats, pulled up in front of us, with an affable smile on its driver. Ajani had a generous smile that brightened his sun-beaten face. Married with his third baby on the way, Ajani we guessed was probably in his late-30s. He shared his home with his in-laws, a few cousins, and us.

Like a long-time friend, we gossiped over our common occurrences with the woman. And further, he told me of his own rare fog incident, similar to mine when I had exited that bus outside of San Marino. Like me, he was cautious about discussing his story with many people. Similar to my experience, the scene he found himself in was astounding – however his story entailed being upon a brilliant mountaintop with a glorious view of several colossal, thunderous waterfalls, where its landing could not be seen. A brilliant sun, glowed its expansive rays upon him, sending him messages he was timid on relating to us. However, when night had fallen, my new companion was able to confide solely in me – perhaps because we were exceptional to others. Like myself, we knew it was our future world.

§

Ajani knew he was no longer walking on the desert, rocky path. He was walking. He assumed he just walked right on into heaven without even realizing it. His feet no longer hurt from the tattered, flat sandals he normally wore. He was unable to feel those ruthless pebbles gnawing into his soles at every step.

His blistered feet began to feel abnormally comfortable, as if having a soothing foot massage while walking at the same time. That was the first feeling he noticed that snapped him into his new surroundings.

He stopped. He looked up. 'Where am I?' he thought. A cool breeze poured upon him instead of the sandy, heat from his familiar home. He looked around. He was on a mountain top, but the land was level at this peak. His view around him was a range of mountains, some covered with snow and others green. At various edges, he viewed breathtaking waterfalls, hearing the lovely crash they made as they hit the lakes below. It was stunning. He had never seen waterfalls before, let alone snow. He knelt down to touch the snow at his bare feet that oddly did not feel a tinge of frostbite one would normally experience. The snow felt cold in his hands, but it had a refreshing sense. He felt the kind sun in the sky looking down upon him. He was drawn to gaze up, with no glare piercing his eyes. The bright sunshine warmed through him.

Something above was sending him a message. The world was changing. He knew that this world, the one he was now standing in, was the world that earth would one day be. Was that right? He wasn't sure. It was either a physical transformation that would occur or it was a world that already existed that human beings would transition into. Whatever the case, he knew he had to share this with someone.

§

We had just left Cape Town and were now journeying to an extreme sun-baked desert area where bone-thin children and adults walked abundant. It was the scene of what the incessant old '80s poverty-stricken US commercials used to display to tug at your heartstrings. But in person, it was surreal. The ridiculous pestering hungry flies made their ways comfortably settling on faces of those too weak to wave them off, sucking whatever more precious blood these unoffending souls had. Those in semi-decent health stood in this offensive heat in winding, long lines for basic food and medicine. It was in this sad village that the remarkable event occurred.

Roman had remained at the hotel we were currently at, calling, busy as usual, handling and taking care of plans for our trip to Greece. My "all business and no fun" companion was a little neurotic at times. I noticed on occasion if he were deeply involved in calculating our assorted income, and if you were to get to close, he would scold back "3 feet, 3 feet..." disliking invasion to his personal space.

Being that our time was filled with interviews and breathing in these unworldly changes, my time with Roman on a personal level was limited. I knew he was married once. No kids. Unclear on the details of his divorce however. He was somewhat of an introvert but quite intelligent and gladly enjoyed discussing intense subjects such as anatomy and economics (which frankly did not interest me in the least).

Roman had left Ajani and me to discuss further our experiences, to see if we could make sense of anything that had been happening to us. We were visiting a friend of Ajani's, chatting outside, when we were interrupted by one of the locals. I could not comprehend him, but this individual was apparently urging folks to follow him, saying, Ajani translated, "Come! Come! This way! Hurry!" the man continued, in his native tongue. We followed the bustling, growing crowd.

We came upon an intense scene. I did not recognize who they were, but I knew from Ajani that they were an unforgiving group. Riding wild horses, they brandished their weapons, intimidating and harassing the locals. A few of the courageous were demanding that they leave their village alone, at peace. I knew, immediately, to them I did not belong, was not wanted; once they spotted me, I would be their aggravated focus. I crept back, trying to dissolve in the crowd. But a yell in my direction was made.

It was then that I saw her. Again. She did not look at us. She was barefoot once more. But with a simple gesture, she laid a hand on the burning sand. We all stood, surrounding her, but no one daring to go within 30 feet of her. The rebels though, it seemed, remained oblivious. Ajani and I looked at each other, stunned. She looked up at us. She spoke no words yet my mind was calmed with words to simply "observe." The same mist engulfed her and she was gone.

We felt a gentle rumbling underneath our feet. The horses were becoming anxious and refused to obey their bitter riders. Like foolish bull riders, the rebels were thrown off the animals and the beasts galloped fast away. Slowly backing away from where she had disappeared, the crowd was making a circular perimeter from her imprint. But the militant group continued on, as if nothing were occurring. They charged at us and the crowd, shooting up a storm. But no bullets fell back, striking any of us. I glanced at Ajani. We were befuddled. The locals were standing next to and some even *through* the volatile group. Neither group however seemed aware of the other. I was confused again. My eyes trying to keep focus of what was happening. I could tell by Ajani's confused squint, he was seeing the same as me.

The sand was becoming moist. Not from fear, but a primal knowing, the crowd backed further. The shouts of the crazed rebels were diminishing. And soon, Ajani and I no longer saw any of them. To us, they had simply... disappeared. It wasn't long until we saw water, clear and fresh, blue and beautiful, make its way to the surface, cooling our sizzling feet and ankles. The water was spreading from where she had left, growing ever so kindly, outwards. It was hollowing out into the ground as well. This small puddle was suddenly emerging into a roomful flood! Still filled with the calm she had blessed upon us, we knowingly made more and more room for this fledgling water. It did not force us away; rather we understood it and let it have its way.

A few of the men had ran off yelling ecstatically back to the rest of the villagers. Ajani and I remained in awe, as the water began to spread and deepen.

"Look!" Ajani pointed. The crowd peered in. We could make out delectable fish – similar to the ones in the region's coastal shores – and other various exotic sea creatures, swimming in this pool. By this time, its growth had lengthened miraculously, that the crowd had moved to the shoreline on our side. People murmured and gasped as it became a small lake, deepening and widening over the massive unlivable dessert.

Lush meadows eventually terminated the advancing waters. We could not see however, in front of us, where it terminated. The lake had grown a few miles in its perimeter. It was only at our feet and to one side we saw the greenery begin to grow. Many of the villagers were crying tears of relief and understanding as they knew now they would be able to live on this food. My companion and I were too dumbfounded to believe what our eyes had just witnessed. However, the locals had not seen, heard, or felt any of what Ajani and I had witnessed; it was as if they had never seen or had immediately forgotten that the militant riders were just a second ago in their presence. Ajani and I remained silent but quickly headed off to find Roman to share yet another peculiar story.

I was happy I did not black out this time and further, that someone else had experienced this along with me. I wasn't crazy!

THIRTEEN

Herrington, Hunter: Terrorist Threat and Firearm Possession.

Nobody really knew of his family background, other than being an only child, having a mother who worked as a waitress at the vulgar pub next door and a father who worked as a factory worker with the town's only surviving manufacturing plant.

He was being forced outside, to the roof. Hunter Herrington, like so many others' tales, was not himself but rather one of his victims. It was a hostage standoff gone badly. He was the leader with this sad, angry group of men following senseless orders. They were demanding money and the release of one of their compatriots. Invading one of the local, small high schools, they were able to gather a small innocent group of students to the roof. The ridiculous band of them thought it was wise to instill the threat of throwing off a student one-by-one to acquire what they wanted.

Hunter was now one of his victims, one of the students. He was just one of the boys. He felt the young man's physique, knew the kid's crushes, the clashes with a few teachers, the number of rebounds he shot at Thursday's basketball game. His mind filled with all the student's facts and passions in his life, absorbing throughout him and engulfing his emotions 100-fold. Hyperventilating, fear permeated all through him, as he was nudged brutally to the edge of the rooftop with Hunter's shotgun. It was cold that day; Autumn was saying goodbye. His body shook from the terror of the gun, the height, the aggressive wind. Goosebumps popped up everywhere. The man was yelling something to the cops below. All he saw were the dizzying parade of red and blue flashes below. One blow was all it took – a horrific screaming as the stern and perilous pavement too quickly pounded violently into his body. Hunter felt it all – the acidic fear in his stomach, the fall that happened to quickly for his mind to dwell on, the brutal impact as his body hit the pavement and the following numbness his body would never overcome. Hunter felt all the physical and mental pain he had caused. He knew, as this boy knew, he would never play ball again.

FOURTEEN

I must have grown accustomed to unbearable heat, for by the time we landed in Greece's summer season, I felt as comfortable as the locals. Roman had wished he had been there, to see what Ajani and I had seen. He was continuing his research, documenting everything and everyone who was experiencing some of these changes. I assumed Roman was just like me, although he was more scientific in trying to come up with any sense to these events. Ajani had been able to accompany us along to this beautiful country, and thanks to Roman, we were able to initially stay in an exotic suite at one of their elegant and extravagant hotels. The room radiated its marble appeal with elegant, gold leaf touches. Its velvet, ornate, pillowy couches washed all our tensions away upon our lounge.

We were here to meet Zarina who had sent a luxury escort to drive us to her astounding home. I had never seen a property expand to at least a quarter of a mile long! Meandering our way past the gated entrance, the unending pathway was lined with fresh, lively coconut and banana trees on either side. I discovered later that half of her family background stemmed from Greece, whereas the other half had Malaysian descent. Gorgeous valentine-pink and lemon-yellow hibiscus filled the gaps between, filling our drive uncommonly with a pleasant fragrance.

Exotic baskets of durian, mangosteen, pineapple, papaya and rambutan, perfumed and greeted us in the open outdoor foyer. Walking past the stone and marble archway, our escort continued to accompany us at our side. Gurgling, a soft welcome, the open courtyard jeweled a sparkling, spherical fountain. Easily accommodating over a couple hundred visitors, the home met us with its wide steps ended at the double-door entrance. The regal doorbell was rung, and shortly, a kind, petite servant invited us in.

A confident and self-assured woman, Zarina eloquently met us in the indoor hall. Speaking close-to-perfect English, she clearly spoke a vibrant, "Hello!" and fully embraced us all into her home. Her charm and appeal, with true sincerity, at once made us feel kindly welcome.

A Mozart sonata soothed its violin medley throughout her home. She was obviously one of those proper hostesses where you hold off on discussing any important matters until your guests were made comfortable. We all chatted superficially about our wonderful journey, the plane ride, where we were all from, and how we all became acquainted with each other. She chipped in her two cents as to how Roman and she came in contact as well.

We savored and polished off the sticky rice and spicy lamb; the taste of the coconut milk was a surprising treat in the Malay cuisine. The ais kacang cooled off and sweetened our dining experience to a filling end.

§

Our nonstop chatter continued on until dawn. Roman, exhausted from his brain cells working overtime, excused himself, as Zarina graciously offered up one of the guest rooms as a place to rest. Ajani, having only been occasionally outside of his village, took this opportunity to enjoy the grounds on her spectacular property.

Zarina and I were left to discuss a fascinating account of hers.

§

Zarina stood alone. She had been in her garden, relaxing and pruning a few of the family's fruit trees in the back. It was only a day ago that reports of the visions of the woman had begun. Actually, she really had not paid much attention to the news about this woman, so she was not quite prepared for what happened. Her medical mind, after this experience, had began to think that possibly there was a tumor growing somewhere in her brain to explain the odd occurrence.

A cloud began to quietly appear around her, surrounding her, like a child playing about to sneak up on you. She was shocked, but not frightened.

All around her, there were an abundant number of flowering and fruit trees. A gorgeous garden of them! Unique and familiar colors, scents new and old – so deep, vibrant, and remarkable – filled her senses! Zarina felt herself a much-traveled woman, and had always made a point to visit botanical institutions to view the country's variety of plants and fruits and flowers. In this state, however, she found herself amongst 40 or 50 fruit and flowering trees, seeing and smelling kinds she knew she had never witnessed before. Not in any of her countless travels had she seen any of these vibrant colors, the strange look of these fruits, the beauty of these flowers.

She found herself in a meditative state, walking through this striking floral patch. She had no inkling of how she arrived here, but had no longing to return home either. She had a sudden realization: This is how earth will be. How it would happen or when it would happen, she was unsure.

She found herself soon back home. But she stood, happy, grateful, knowing that that spellbound environment would soon return.

§

I sat stunned. "So what do you make of it?" I curiously asked.

She gave a polite shrug. "Who knows? Heaven on earth?" She joked? I wasn't sure. Well, after everything that had happened, why couldn't that be possible?

I told her of Ajani's and my experiences – witnessing the earthquake, the dessert, the future. Roman had obviously related some of these events to her; however, she respectfully listened to my side of the story. Smiling, she seemed to make sure no one was around. *Someone* in particular? We walked outdoors through the open, wide French doors, to a stone and brick patio. A maze and mix of potted plants and vibrant flowers grew neatly, smartly positioned throughout the backyard landscape. We sat at a stone bench, momentarily admiring the colorful view. Zarina had her butler attend to us with lemonades (or what tasted like lemonade anyway).

"Your home is really beautiful," I complimented.

"Thank you... This is actually the house I've grown up in. My parent's home... They're busy with their traveling..." she continued, explaining the couple's retirement.

"Oh I thought it was yours and your husbands?" assuming maybe she was married.

Embarrassed, she shook her head. "Too busy with medicine perhaps?" After medical school, Zarina became immersed with the radiology program at the hospital and eventually specialized in that field.

"How long have you known Dr. Montecchio?" she asked quite out-of-the-blue. Was she really *interested* in a fussy little man like him? I found himself actually growing a tinge jealous.

"Oh Roman? ...Hmm... Not that long. A few months maybe?" He wasn't too sure. He rarely communicated with Roman, even during their long stay in South Africa.

"You're not then close with him?" she asked. Did she mean *close* "close"? Or just a *friends* "close"?

"He's becoming a good friend. I didn't get to spend that much time with him though when we visited Ajani. Ajani and I were too busy trying to come to some explanation to these strange phenomenons."

She seemed relieved, but still continued on. "And... so... what do you think of him?"

I wasn't too sure what she was alluding to. Did Roman say something, do something, to waver her trust? "Umm... He's fine I guess. He can be pretty finicky. A little neurotic," I laughed, guessing that that was what she was alluding to.

Her eyes brightened a little. "Yes." But there seemed to be something else. Zarina felt very comfortable with Tanner. "I don't know..." There was something she couldn't put her finger on, but her trust in Roman was a little unstable. "Do you trust him?" she asked secretly.

I had never thought about it. Why? Was Roman the type *not to* trust? "Well..." giving it a moment to ponder, "He's never really made me think otherwise. ... Why do you ask?"

"...Hmm... Not sure, Tanner..." She paused; Zarina wasn't one of those people who liked to boast. "I'm just usually a good judge of character. There is something about Roman. ... Is he really a doctor?" she questioned.
"I believe so... Well, Charlie – good friend of mine – was the one who introduced me to him.

I don't think he'd befriend anyone untrustworthy."

She pursed her lips, unsure. "Well... perhaps it's nothing..." and shrugged it off. "Anyhow!" She changed the subject wanting to know more about me instead. "You teach right?"

"Mmmhhmm..." I nodded, taking a sip of the cool drink. "Yes... A few English classes."

"I've always wanted to study English..." I knew she meant focusing on writing, rather than the language. "...But my family's always wanted to carry on the medical tradition."

"It's a respected field. Demanding too." I didn't recall much from my general requirements days of Biology and Chemistry.

"That it is. ... When –" She went to continue further, but we were interrupted by a sudden noise in the distance and a sudden overcast sky shadowing over us.

It sounded like a low rumbling. I couldn't tell if there was some odd noise coming from some *thing* or if it was from the distant thunder? But the noise was becoming more intense. A light drizzle started to pour on us, quickly turning into a fierce downpour in under a minute. We started to run back inside. Zarina grabbed my arm as we found ourselves becoming surrounded in a haze and instantly knew something strange was to occur.

I stood firmly on the ground. No earthquake going on, but why did I hear the rumbling? The fog was dissipating. We stood arm in arm, but took a deep breath as we found ourselves discovering that we were no longer in Zarina's beautiful home.

At first, all we could hear and make sense of was gunfire in the air. Men were running everywhere; some in citizens clothing, others in military gear. The horrendous rain was blurring all our vision. It was some kind of civil dispute we found ourselves in the middle of. They didn't see us, it seemed. Were we invisible to them? What's more, how did we end up here? And exactly where was *here*?

The angry combatants heard the rumbling too. Some of them paid attention, but most did not – until the noise became louder. Again, the earth began to shake, but oddly – Zarina and I remained firm. It seemed as if we were *watching* the scene. The men looked at the ground standing back. A break in the earth was developing. The crack enlarged, growing from a few feet to a mile long. It was hard to make out at first, because the fracture was causing so much smoke and dirt to fill the air. But furiously a jagged mound could be seen rising from the split.

A frightened fighter was seen caught on something, as the growing mountain arose from the earth. He was being pulled up along with it. I desperately wanted to help him, seeing his terrified face. I reached out to grab him, yelling for him to stretch his arm out to me. I assumed he wasn't listening to me because he didn't speak English. I jumped up, trying to grab his leg at least. But – my hand simply went *through* him! Shocked, I gasped… It was again as if there were two worlds occurring right before my eyes. I glanced to my side to see Zarina, as she stood stunned along with me. The panicked man finally lost his hold as the mountain was now not only towering over 100 feet, but the downpour was creating slippery mud slides on its surface. Like a rag doll, he fell limply downwards, his body awkwardly hitting and bumping against the merciless rocks. I felt the sickening knots in my stomach. *Breathe...* Why was I seeing this? Why was it like we were in a different dimension?

The mountain continued to erupt from the earth, tearing the land in half, forcing it's massiveness to divide the extreme insurgents. The shouts of all involved that were once filled with anger towards their enemies were now turned to shouts of fear for their own lives. But the mountain reacted unforgivingly, growing skywrds and pushing the fighters aside. Minutes passed... 15.... 20... Half an hour... I lost track as to when the violent noise of the angry eruption finally settled down. But when all was finished, the mountain had reached over 30 miles long, over 5000 feet tall. It was as if God himself had said, 'If you can't make up your mind on how to share and divide the land, I'll do it for you.'

We became engulfed in white… and were back at Zarina's lovely backyard momentarily, the sun once again shining brightly.

It took us both awhile to comprehend just exactly what had happened. This wasn't my first time of having these bi-worldly experiences, but it was Zarina's first. So it took her more than a few minutes to come out of the deer-in-the-headlights look.

"…what… what was that?" she attempted to find a seat to lower herself on.

"I'm still not sure. ... Since that experience with Ajani, I've been trying to make sense of it ever since."

She was now sitting on a cushioned, lounge chair, but gripping the sides as if another mist would come again and transport her to another bizarre scene. I tried to help her calm down further with my meditative breathing lessons.

"Goodness... That was just..." She was still trying to bring herself back to reality... if this even was reality.

"Do you have any idea where we were?" I had briefly recalled hearing the men there speaking a language which I thought was similar to hers.

She seemed to concentrate on my question. After coming to what she thought was the answer, she headed back indoors in search of this morning's paper. She didn't have to search for whatever it was for very long. It was the main story on the front page. An article discussed the latest progress (if any) on a civil dispute occurring in some northern region. She began to explain to me the background details of a militant group harassing some rural citizens, how there was a stubborn dispute on land ownership. But my eyes were focused on the article's main picture. It looked like the scene that Zarina and I had just left. I could swear that one of the men, in the picture, standing as a passenger in the background jeep was the same one I had tried to rescue from that rising, enraged mountain.

Zarina suddenly turned on her TV set. Of course – there had to be some news about a growing mountain coming out of the ground!

I was glued to the TV as feelings of what I had felt back in the hospital all came back to me. The TV reported: nothing. In fact, there wasn't even any news of the civil dispute's progress. That was odd. Zarina spoke my same sentiment aloud, "Why isn't there even any update on the fight?"

"Mmhhmm…" I agreed. I sat down next to her as our eyes remained fixed, waiting for any breaking news.

Roman walked in the room. He had woken up from his nap. We began to talk excitedly about what had just happened to us and how there was no verification on the news. He listened as well as he could with the sleepiness still in his face. He wrinkled his brows, with a groggy, "…really?…" Grabbing for the newspaper, I went to show him the picture of the scene we had just left. But I was speechless. Zarina, seeing my reaction, asked a quick "what?" and saw the same image on the front paper. There was no story on the civil controversy. Instead, what was shown was some random story about a new merger between a small technology company and its international competitor. We rummaged through the paper. Surely it was in here. But it was quite clear something strange was once again occurring. We briefly went berserk wondering if we were still in the same year. But Roman confirmed to us, quizzically, brought us back to earth confirming that we were still in the same day.

How was it possible? Why were we not seeing any story on this struggle? Why was there no story about it on the news? What had just happened? Zarina and I decided to keep everything to ourselves (with the exception of Ajani who didn't doubt *any* of our experience for a second). We didn't want anyone thinking we were going mad.

We stayed in her home for a few weeks, all of us taking our time in really getting to know each other and what we wanted to accomplish – if anything – out of our new troupe. Roman was always ready and willing to suggest and guide us in whatever approaches we threw out. We simply needed to understand what was happening to us, why the three of us were seeing bizarre things, and what it all meant. For now, we decided we would just continue trying to locate others like us.

FIFTEEN

I wasn't sure how, but a few of the locals actually discovered what had happened to Zarina and I. We all decided to head out to Athens for a tour around the "Sanctuary of Olympian Zeus". It was a deathly heat-stricken day. We were appreciating the beauty of the place when I noticed a piece of paper was suddenly thrown near my feet. But since I was standing near a public trash can, I thought that whoever it was had just missed the basket. But then a few more garbage was thrown our way. I turned to see what was going on. There was a group of 6 or 7 young men and women; they apparently seemed to know who we were. At first, taken aback, we side-stepped the light trash being thrown towards us, but it was when their objects became fiercer that things began to happen.

One of the taller men in the group threw a hard baseball-size rock our way. And, I could see it ready to brutally strike Zarina near the temple. I attempted to block it, but ... something else stopped it.

The rock simply dropped.

At first it was barely noticed, but when the biblical rock-throwing commenced, a wall of their rocks reached within a foot of us and dropped. It was as if we were protected by a loving force field. The three of us gathered closer together. People began to assemble, noticing that something was transpiring. All in the crowd briefly backed away, but more so to distance themselves from those that were throwing the rocks. The nasty group was taken aback and instantly released any items that were intended to be shot our way.

A combination of silence and shrieks and cries of fear and forgiveness instantly followed. They were looking beyond us and quickly ran off. I turned around. I saw nothing.

Slowly, kindly, some other tourists came up to us. "Are you ok?" with fellow observers remarking, "What was that for?"

"Thank you... Yes... I--" I shrugged my shoulders, "I have no... I don't know why..." I looked over at Zarina who was obviously more irritated than scared. Swearing in her tongue, she was carrying on a hyper conversation with a considerate woman. She would yell in the direction those idiots had run off in. After some people rejected it as some kids having nothing better to do, the three of us were eventually left on our own.

Ajani looked at us gently, laying a calm, tight clasp upon our hands. "They're scared of you." He honestly said. "They're scared of *us*." he corrected. But the few who knew what had happened to Zarina and I didn't also know about Ajani. Or did they? I hadn't noticed if trash had been thrown near his feet as well.

"We did not do anything to them!" Zarina was still very upset about it. No one had ever disrespected her before.

I tried to reason out what Ajani had honestly just spoken. "People don't know what to make of us. We don't even know what to make of us! We'll just have to be sure that we keep things more to ourselves."

"But we did not even tell anyone *anything*!" She defended.

I couldn't explain. All I could say was, "I know... I know..." She was right. Who had told?

§

It was a quiet rode home. I never did find out what those people had seen behind us. I distracted my thoughts by turning on the radio, but again, there was more news of earthly changes. As a blessing – or was it a hoax? – There was recent scientific research claiming the ozone layer effects were astoundingly reversing! Was it possible? There were also more personal claims about the fog and how it was changing people. And also how it was not changing people. There were claims of people disappearing – which I found absurd to hear. Could the top leaders of every government have secretly gathered together and put together a strategy to straighten out crime and improper behavior? But I didn't think that would have been possible. When did these leaders even have the time to strategize a scheme like that? ...Maybe I really was insane.

Stories about these disappearances though were growing daily. They seemed to either only affect innocent people, like children and infants, or the people who had had a so-called "bad" experience in that mysterious fog, and yet managed to express genuine remorse. Why hadn't I yet then "disappeared"? Or did I even *want to* disappear?

SIXTEEN

Cortez, Rodrigo: Arson and Firearm Possession.

It was a ridiculous dispute between rival gangs. They were in a forgotten warehouse near the city's lake. Rodrigo was no longer himself; he became Manuel – one of the latest members in the rival gang to be initiated in. The gunshots were firing pointlessly like a video game gone mad in this abandon building. Complete regret overtook him as he questioned why he had felt the need to join them. They had harassed him saying that he would always be able to rely on his *hermanos*, but this chaos left him feeling more and more alone. Something hit near him. He was taken aback by the pop of Rodrigo's bullet that had shot past him, he hadn't noticed the fire begin rising. Later reports could not determine if it was the ancient furnace or a bad transformer that caused the fire. He couldn't outrun it; he couldn't escape. Things began collapsing all around him, cornering him. He felt the heat, the anger of the fire, inevitably working his way around him. His skin began to blister, as he screamed from the pain of his skin setting afire and suffocation of the smoke.

Rodrigo would later tell me the pain of that fire would linger on his body for days later.

SEVENTEEN

The earth was growing quiet. For awhile now, it had been happening. I don't think people gave it much thought, but I noticed it with one of the first odd news reports – an infamous zoo in Thailand reported a majority of its animals had quite simply disappeared. Many folks dismissed it as a prank by a crazed animal rights group, although that lead went unresolved. Every time I looked out into the midday sky, I noticed the sound becoming more muted. The birds were vanishing. Some weeks later I heard more and more reports of the missing animals. Zoos, jungles, safaris, friends of the entomologists and even man's best friend from normal households – all were slowly becoming mysteriously more and more absent.

Ajani had heard from his family back home about news of a well-known malevolent tribe; they were making their faces less publicized. However, it was due to the fact that the members were gradually disappearing, and there was a brief speculation that they were being silently murdered. But no proof was found to confirm that. And we all knew and felt that that honestly wasn't what was happening. As the tribes' murderous leaders began to vanish, its cowardly disbanded members began fearing that they were next. They either ended up running around profusely begging for apologies to their gods or to their victims, or they felt an imminent fate approaching and ultimately would beat death to its punch.

Back home in the States, I also had heard of some disappearances. Jails were becoming silent. Like the confused members of that

African tribe, the guards and other correctional officers were initially concerned the inmates were escaping somehow. But they, as well, knew that that truly wasn't the answer. A few officers took note and tried to summarize who and which prisoners remained. They had fallen into two categories: those that were innocently committed or those that had sincerely repented.

I was so confused! I thought I had finally figured it all out: Only good people disappeared or only bad people disappeared. But in my eyes, it seemed as if both were occurring. It made no sense to me.

It was rare that one would actually *witness* a disappearance. Although those that claimed to have seen someone vanish would describe it as a molecular diminishing. One father in Bolivia had written about his newborn's departure.

"15-March: Eduardo was a noticeable 4 kilograms at birth. He was only with us for 2 days before he disappeared. ... I was holding him when he it happened. I felt his body becoming lighter and lighter. And when I look down, I see that he is fading, like he is becoming like a ghost." The report on this man's account, however, was never confirmed. His written account had been simply found on a rocking chair.

EIGHTEEN

Ajani left today.

Unusually alone, we had been discussing Roman's itinerary for our upcoming visit to New Zealand. He had made plans for us to meet another one of his acquaintances. I was excited about going to a new country, so I didn't notice him at first. ..Ajani was oddly calm.. Quiet.. Eerie at first. I thought he was on the verge of passing out or something, and I suggested that we take a break. And like the image of those wise old men who look at you with some *knowing* that you foolishly do not know of, he smiled at me and took my hand. Strangely, I felt myself losing his grasp. ..His hand floated through mine... And the imprint of his thoughts upon mine was that he was '*I'm still here…*' – yet physically, he was gone.

NINETEEN

Another plane, another new country...

Zarina decided to continue on and join Roman
and I on the next step of our journey. She
generously supplied our travel arrangements;
we flew on a business, luxury midsize jet that
Zarina's family had recently bought. Used
more for entertainment, however, the plane
wasn't accustomed to flying long distances.
With Zarina supplying the vehicle, Roman was
more than capable of handling all the other
details of where we would need to stopover
and fill up this gorgeous aircraft. Only six large
comfortable, tan-colored chairs and two
loveseat-style sofas, facing each other, graced
the interior. Mini-TV monitors sat near most
chairs, along the window counter. A few large
table trays were easily raised for your use;

Roman had a ton of papers spread about on one, busily writing as usual.

Zarina was resting, so I took this time to open my journal and review over and write down what I had encountered so far.

"...Literally felt divided, in half. ...Dizzy... Saw terrible thing happen – collapse of church and historical museum. Tanner there! But did not see any of it. Why???..." A few entries later, "...Crazy thing happened in village!!! Saw her again today! Was standing in sand with group. She touched the ground. Water began appearing! It grew into a huge lake!" I thought back to that day... how miraculous that lake had come about. I continued reading, "...Met Zarina (beautiful, passionate, ladylike...)... Z & I saw mountain erupt out of the ground!!! Saw *her!!! She spoke somehow – telepathically??? Said to just "observe"!!* Was able to not get dizzy this time! No news of it anywhere! It's as if the civil battle <u>never even existed</u>!" … "People are disappearing. Seem to fall into a category of *good people*. Maybe we're slowly being taken away to heaven???" The words sent goosebumps up my spine. "Confused… disappearances are continuing. Seems now it's what some would see as *bad people*. Doesn't make any sense. Where are we all going???" I read over my words over and over and over. Somewhere in the distance, I heard the pilot announce a refuel stop.

I thought about all these people in my life: Charlie, Ajani, Zarina, Roman. I thought about what I had experienced with each. …I glanced over at Zarina… then at Roman. … I now understood.

TWENTY

Dr. Anna Micelli

Back and forth, back and forth, back and forth... She had a bad habit of swinging her legs when she was nervous. Her mom would jokingly sit fat Gladys, the young, family Lab, on her little legs when her swinging would start. It was no fun spending the remaining days of summer vacation at the hospital. The awkward days of Fifth Grade were fast approaching.

Anna found herself in this child's body. She had been here before. St. Anthony's Hospital – the first hospital she worked at during her residency upon graduating from UMB.

The woman was wheeling her kindly in the bumpy wheelchair. She was nervous. Anxious.

Worried. Her mind told her there was a simple operation up ahead. The resident was kind though, easing her nerve-wracked brain. She would talk to her about others who already successfully had the operation. She was optimistic, but not to the point where her words were filled with fake and forced enthusiasm. Before entering the surgical doors, she took a moment to really talk to me and lean in to embrace me sweetly.

I thanked her looking up at her glowing, understanding face. I laughed, aware of what was occurring, seeing my reflection.

TWENTY-ONE

Roman had always held a pessimistic view of the world, always in competition with others, always believing that there was a way to make a quick buck no matter what poor soul got in the way. He was not a man who liked change. Abhorred it, actually.

He looked over at the two of them. Laughing… Smiling… They really cared about each other. …Shame he had to get rid of them. He watched her laugh at his ridiculous stories. He remembered a laugh like that. He once told such ridiculous stories. Her smile reminded him of…her. …Aida.

Aida and he had been so happy – they were engaged! She had said "yes"! Together they didn't look like much (appearance-wise especially) but to Roman that never mattered at all. It hadn't bothered him at all they had only known each other barely three months before he proposed. And she was stunned. Thrilled! So he thought.

The two of them were immediately caught up in wedding plans. He wanted a grand wedding. She wasn't sure what she wanted just yet. On the other hand, he knew exactly what he wanted: yellow roses, 300 of his closest family and friends (in Roman's case, this would be mainly 'acquaintances'), 10 groomsmen in white tuxes and 10 bridesmaids in pewter dresses (design could be selected by his bride...maybe), Aida in ivory, titanium wedding bands, a double-breasted white tux, ceremony at St. Anna's church, and a relaxing, two-week honeymoon in Maldives. He was ecstatic! She was...not. Roman couldn't understand why. He dismissed it to engagement jitters, but Aida was changing. She was more – edgy? He didn't really know. But after months into their engagement and of Aida growing more irritable, he was determined to figure out what was really going on.

He began to do what he was so good at – sleuth around. He followed her one day after pretending to leave for the office. He wanted to see what she was up to in a typical day since she was in between jobs. It was a few hours later until she headed out. He took control of his car. She was driving somewhere. Minutes later, they were driving into the adjacent city. He wasn't familiar with this town. Where was she driving? She made so many turns as they entered the city's downtown area. The buildings began looking older and more miserable at every turn she took. She finally pulled into a back hidden parking area of an old apartment building. For a second he thought he may have been following someone else and had mistakenly ended up following someone else that drove a car similar to Aida's. She was sitting in her car, nonchalant. A few minutes later, a half-shaven, skinny man exited the building's back door. He was wearing a dirty white T-shirt, tattered denims, an old pair of sandals, with a cigarette hanging out of his mouth needing to be extinguished. It was a sad sight what he saw next. The man just mumbled a "...hey..." to her and slipped her something into her extended hand, displaying some folded up bills. Roman's stomach sickened. '...why?....' he thought. She didn't say anything to him but just took what she had driven there for and left.

Unbeknownst to Roman, Aida never was the type to handle stress well. She was nearing 40. And when she met Roman, she never thought it would lead to anything. When he had proposed, her answer was a reply more in desperation than anything. Poor guy – he was clueless. She wasn't at all attracted to this scrawny man. She always dreamed and fantasized of a strong and striking man to rescue her away from her scullery and housemaid duties. Her response to Roman's proposal was such an automatic, impulsive answer, she probably would've said "yes" to a frog if it had asked.

Roman had tried to do a kindly intervention, after discovering Aida's new bad habits. But Aida was one of those girls who quickly got annoyed with "nice guys." So Roman's type of confrontation fizzled flat. For days on end, the two would continue to bicker until it escalated to the predictable outcome – their engagement was called off. She was relieved. He was depressed.

Not being able to get completely over her, he would frequently continue stalking her. She was working at a new home for a journalist. Another man arrived months later to live with this researcher. His anal, obsessive-compulsive brain set to work. He wanted to find out more about these gentlemen. The other man had a substance abuse past as well. The fanatic neurons ran frantic in his head. *This man* contributed to his ex-beloved's use. This man would have to pay.

As he casually introduced himself to Charlie, he knew it would eventually lead him to Tanner. The man, he thought, was even more disturbed – talking of strange worldly changes along with the other freaks out there. Roman never witnessed any of these things. This man was evil, he concluded. His intellect reasoned – the world would do a lot of good to be rid of Tanner Reed.

§

Roman was a man scorned and gone irrational. He had become determined to clean out anyone associated with Tanner and anyone making ungodly claims about seeing some blasphemous world events. His neurotic mind justified that he was doing the world a service getting rid of this new evil in the world. When Charlie confided in him of Tanner and his pill discovery, he already knew this was 'victim number one.' Then, through his various connections, he set out to draw to him others interested in discovering more on the woman. Roman, always a believer that others were more prone to deceit like him, senselessly believed that the ones who responded to him had selfish intentions as well. When Ajani Mbele contacted him, he knew he had found 'victim number two.' Ajani came from a small village, so he assumed it was this man's way of either getting out of his poverty or gaining wealth for his own family or just simply needed to be eliminated for his insane claims. Zarina Azalia contacted him a few days later. From running a background search on her, he discovered that this was a woman very well off financially, so he only assumed she must naturally be seeking notoriety in her practice. He wasn't really sure what her motive was but since she had obviously fallen for Tanner and was making ridiculous claims as well, she became: Victim number three.

It didn't take long for him to slowly gather these individuals together. Meanwhile, his three dupes would continue their nonsensical babbling. He continued to never actually witness any of their ridiculous claims so his damaged heart told him they were being just as deceitful as him.

TWENTY-TWO

His resolute hand showed no backing down. How had it come to this? Their plane hand landed not more than 10 minutes ago and here Roman now stood, with the weapon pointed ominously at Zarina and him. We clashed in disharmony to the splendor of the landscape.

The plane had landed in an isolated strip. All around us we could see nothing but hilly dense forests, and in the distance stood a few snow-topped mountains. I would've been absorbed in the beauty had Roman not yet shocked us with this sudden change. He had already generously paid and allowed the pilot to leave early before turning into Mr. Hyde.

Zarina and I had been rising out of our seats, extending our tired legs, when we heard the cock of the gun. We had been busy laughing about a silly childhood story from Zarina's past that we were completely caught off guard seeing Roman's face change from his usual look of a frenzied accountant to one of a sinister assassin.

"…what…" I was too frozen to continue, Zarina as well. Was he joking around?

Roman, noticing something out the window, snapped, "GET OUT!" He waved the gun angrily towards the plane door. I held onto Zarina's arm as we headed to the door. I saw a car pull up near the plane. A familiar face beamed up at us. Charlie!

He was yelling up to us about Roman wanting to surprise us with his visit. I wanted to grab Zarina and make a run for it, but it didn't seem as if there would be a hospital for miles around if one of us were to get shot. I don't know if

Charlie saw the fear in our faces first or saw Roman's gun, but I noticed his face quickly change from joy to shock. My friend was out of his vehicle by the time Roman had appeared – Roman timing everything just right – at the plane's doorway, with the gun still pointing straight at us.

Charlie made no move forward and stood dumbfounded. "...Roman?... What's going on?" We continued walking cautiously down the steps to the pavement.

Roman, continued to command us from behind, "Over there!" shoving us towards Charlie.

Charlie was starting to raise his hands in defense and puzzlement, bravely asking, "...This a joke?... What's going on?" He looked from Roman to us for any clue. I gave Charlie an honest shrug, expressing that I was as just confused as he was. Zarina stood tight against me, not like I could stop a bullet though if it decided to head our way.

"I was planning this..." The crazy man was laughing, continuing, "You ruined my life Tanner!"

Now I was really confused. "Me??"

He went on, his attention to Zarina, saying, "Aida and I were happy until your *boyfriend* messed it all up!" Who was Aida? The only Aida I could think of was the maid at Charlie's house.

"My housekeeper?!" Charlie screamed, reading my thoughts.

"Charlie here told me about finding that pill."
What pill?

Tanner recalled Aida. He had dismissed it before. He thought she had just had a fun, drunken night out with friends the night before. He could hear Charlie making some defense in the background about some blue pills he had seen on the floor. Tanner should have known – Aida's behavior was once his behavior.

Tanner mumbled "...Aida..." unconsciously, with Charlie catching it quickly. He saw Charlie's face twist in angst about the mistaken identity.Charlie realized – it hadn't been Tanner's pill at all! It was Aida's.

"...oh God..." Charlie mumbled. With his furrowed brows, he gave me an apologetic look. His body crumpled with shame, from his false accusation. "…I told Roman about some blue pill I found in my house. …I figured it was yours?"

I shook my head. "…no… I just finished rehab Charlie. You know I'm over that." I was momentarily hurt that my friend wouldn't believe I had conquered my addiction.

Charlie looked at me with true apology. I didn't blame him. It wasn't his fault. He hadn't known Aida was Roman's ex-fiancé. He could see now why she had left this obsessed little man.

Roman seemed to disregard the whole misunderstanding. His stubborn mind refused to believe that Tanner was legit. He stuck to his beliefs that Tanner was still using, corrupted his ex, and was so affected by his use that it was a possible explanation as to why he was able to see such absurd things.

The gun fired.

TWENTY-THREE

The bullet aimed towards Charlie first.

It seemed to take a lifetime for the shell to reach him. But Zarina and I stood back in surprise as we could see Charlie's body slowly disappearing. Molecularly, he was dissolving. Charlie knew he was safe.

Our eyes turned towards Roman. He looked wild with insanity. And remarkably, he didn't seem to notice Charlie vanishing at all!! The gun was next pointed to Zarina. I gulped nervously – Roman was saving me for last. I watched as Zarina began to fade away as well! I briefly wondered where she now stood.

The dark, endless hole of the gun finally faced my way. I nervously fidgeted, having nowhere to run, my friends all gone. I was too distracted to hear what he was saying, but I knew Roman was yelling at me being evil and demonic and that I would now stop seeing my bogus visions. I heard the jolting blare of the bullet release. I knew it was coming my way. I shut my eyes. ... I began to feel myself growing lighter. I felt my body floating away.

TWENTY-FOUR

I had realized what had finally happened. After opening my eyes, I was still standing in the same place. I was still standing on that pavement. What's more, my friends were there with me as well – looking as astonished as me.

Tanner spoke an agreeable, "…Whoa…"

Zarina's eyes shone as she saw me. We laughed, exhaling a "Wow!" as we embraced.

We understood where we were. This pristine world was marvelous.

TWENTY-FIVE

As I had realized back on the plane, *before* Roman had gone berserk, I had reached what could only be the logical conclusion of what had been happening to me, Zarina, and Ajani. We were witnesses – observers to *two* different worlds. I now believed we were physically in this *new* world, but had previously been living and viewing both our *old* world and this *new* world. That was the only explanation I could think of when being able to see those contrasting responses of people during all those momentous transformations. When I had seen Charlie and those children, they had been protected, momentarily residing in the *new* world. But now, we had completely transferred over into this *new* world. And those who remained on our *old* world were completely unaware that there were these two different worlds. I can only assume that I was unable to help that unfortunate man as he lost his grasp because we both stood in separate worlds. I guess it depended on our own perspective and that's the environment that ultimately surrounded us.

§

My journal remained, written with my summations, on their side. Hopefully someone would not disregard it. I hoped it could be ultimately used as a book of learning, an understanding to follow, so perhaps one day they could join us on this new earth as well.

Is this new world 100% different? No. there's still some minor disputes that occasionally take place throughout our society. This new world would be quite dull if we still didn't have unique and varying, individual opinions. But has it improved? Definitely. It is the rebirth of our old world.

I still cannot say whether this was an angelic or alien intervention. I only could conclude that our treatment to our fellow man, when all is said and done, affected our future existence. Perhaps it was some divine interference giving us a quick slap to the back of our heads to wake us up. Or was it just time now for our species to progress to a higher level? Was it now our turn for humanity to advance and adapt to a new environment? It was maybe time for mankind to evolve.

FRUITION

He sat in his comfortable office. The floor-to-
ceiling windows welcomed the midday sun.
The quiet hum of the bamboo fans hushed
above. One wall encased a complete bookcase
of his beloved journals, articles, books – some
of which displayed his authored signature. A
set of picture frames on an adjacent wall
electronically blinked random shots of his
grown family. A recent shot of a young man in
a familiar cap and gown blinked on for a few
seconds and vanished. His grandson was
arriving today, from back home; he himself
hadn't returned home to the States since the
woman's initial visits.

He set his coffee down, allowing it to cool a bit
more. Tanner gazed out his window, soaking
in the world he now called home. They had
moved an hour's drive from Zarina's old

family home to a classy, yet comfortable, place near the shore. The scene did not display a horrendous mountain. Rather, a serene hillside with vineyards a few miles in the distance and a calm ocean with its usual fisherman gazed back at him,

He was getting ready to celebrate his birthday. It was hard to believe all those crazy events occurred almost eighty years ago. This new environment was astounding. It was not uncommon to hear of folks living beyond 160 years nowadays. It was a more relaxed, peaceful environment. Disputes were still heard of but only fleeting moments. Countries were still changing in their leadership roles. Every month, it wasn't unusual to hear of news of a country declaring a change to its governmental style. More and more, it transitioned into *groups* of individuals or "advisors" that were becoming political leaders. It wasn't for everyone though. Some nations still preferred and remained comfortable with the old ways, and it worked for them (as well as others).

Occasionally, Zarina, Ajani and Tanner would be able to witness briefly bits of the old world. When those individuals would see them, most screamed in fear thinking we were ghosts. As Tanner later realized however, their new plane of existence resided oddly a few inches above our old world's existence. Thus, it produced the illusion of them *floating* in front of them. The new world itself was not the only thing rising; new facilities were being built to handle individuals experiencing new abilities – it was as if brain use was rising as well. Brain power had always been used at 100%; it was now however advancing, growing to some higher evolved level. Telepathic and telekinetic blips would occur in a common individual, so these new facilities were built to understand how to develop these techniques to a more controlled status. Civilization was progressing.

The office door opened. He joined his cherished friends in celebration.

§